Loretta Browne

This is the third book in the Sadie series inspired by all the hard-working charity workers everywhere!

Dedicated to the best Aunty in the World – Aunty Gail!

Bessie, who lived next door to Sadie, worked in a Charity shop on a Saturday morning. The shop raised money for the Cat Rescue Centre. Bessie loved cats and so did Sadie.

Sadie and her little sister Daisy, looked forward to going to the shop with Aunty Gail. They liked the toy corner and often gave Bessie some of their own books and toys to sell.

One Saturday, Sadie spotted a bike hanging on the wall. It had a blue basket and a little bell. Bessie said that the bike was waiting for a new home.

3

Sadie wished she could have a new bike. Even though it was second hand, it was still too much money for dad. He had just paid out lots of money to fix the roof.

4

Sadie asked Aunty Gail why everything cost so much money. Aunty Gail said that the best things in life were often free. Sadie thought hard about that in the car on the way home.

Miss Rose told the children about the school Summer Fayre. She asked Sadie and her best friend Una to think of an idea for a stall of their own.

Sadie remembered Bessie's shop and the toy section. Sadie and Una agreed on a toy stall but with a difference!

'We would like to have a Swap Shop' Sadie told Miss Rose. 'Children can bring their old toys that they don't play with any more and swap them for a toy from the stall. That way they won't need any money'.

Miss Rose thought the stall sounded terrific. Sadie and Una worked hard over the next few weeks making posters and banners for the stall. Aunty Gail and Daisy helped too.

Sadie told dad that she would like to take her old bike to the stall. Dad and his workmate Bill, cleaned it up and made it look like new. Secretly, Sadie hoped she would be able to swap her trike for a bigger bike at the Fayre.

Sadie spoke to Grandma in Australia. She told Grandma that she felt worried in case nobody came to the stall. Grandma said not to worry and that hard work always pays off. Sadie knew that she always tried her best.

Grandma   Australia

Bessie had made a pretty gingham tablecloth for the stall and Aunty Gail had special hats and T shirts made for Sadie and Una to wear.

Sadie and Una were amazed at how many children came to their stall and swapped their pre-loved toys.

Una swapped her old scooter for one that looked brand new!

14

It was very nearly time to close the Fayre. Sadie felt disappointed because no one seemed to want her trike and no one had brought a bike to swap either. 15

Just then, Bessie arrived at the stall. She was wheeling a bike with a little blue basket. Sadie recognised it from the Charity shop!

16

'I wonder if I could swap this two wheeler bike for that lovely trike?' she asked. Sadie was amazed. She had her new bike after all and it hadn't cost her a penny!

The Summer Fayre had been a great success. Miss Rose donated any left over toys to Bessie's shop and all the profits to the Cat Rescue Centre. Bessie was delighted!

After the Fayre, Dad and Daisy came to pick Sadie up in Uncle Brendan's truck.

Sadie showed dad the bike. 'Well I never! Hard work really does pay off!' said dad.

20

Printed in Great Britain
by Amazon

67425216R00015